A TASTE OF SICILY

ESCAPE TO ITALY

HOLLY GREENE

CONTENTS

CHAPTER 1

"Sicily?" Olivia Bennett narrowed her eyes at her features editor and annoyedly blew a strand of hair out of her face. "Come on, Erica, you can't be serious..."

"Why not?" her colleague replied. "Sicily is beautiful—especially in the spring. *You* get to sit in the sun, eat loads of Italian food, and come back fifteen pounds heavier. Who *wouldn't* want to do that?"

"Me, actually," Olivia responded, irritated. "The place is packed full of tourists, ugly beaches and pushy men. And *everything* smells like fish."

"Jeez," Erica rolled her eyes, "did somebody from the island kick your dog or something?"

Olivia held her tongue and stared past Erica out the window.

Four years before coming to *The Wanderer*, one of the USA's premier travel magazines, she'd started her brand new travel-writing career by following her then-publisher Richard on what was supposed to be a grand tour of Sicily—and double up as a romantic holiday for them too. Excited for a shot at romance and set on finding the hidden gems of Italy, she eagerly accepted the offer.

But three days later, she found herself alone on a Sicilian beach vomiting undercooked garlic prawns and unable to find a decent area on the island that wasn't a tourist trap.

When she finally got home, broken-hearted and miserable, she'd almost considered giving up travel writing altogether. Or at least anything vaguely related to Italy, which was forever soured in her mind.

Snapping back to reality, she turned her gaze to Erica and sighed.

"I just—I thought I might've earned a little bit of leeway, I guess."

Erica had recruited Olivia to *The Wanderer* based on her large established online following, and evocative articles on East Asia, South America, and the Middle East.

Her first assignment for *The Wanderer*, an exploration of glaciers in Patagonia, had been hailed as revolutionary and was already generating buzz for a slew of awards.

But Sicily was quickly becoming the *it* place in Europe for American vacationers, and the combination of a hyped location, and popular writer was just too enticing to pass up.

"Look," Erica conceded, "I know this isn't ideal. But we need our best talent to cover the trendy regions. And Sicily truly is *it* this year. We've gotten hundreds of enquiries about this self-taught chef running a cooking class there that's supposed to be incredible. And I need *you* to check it out to see what the hype is all about."

She slid a glossy paper brochure towards Olivia. On the cover was a photo of a woman in her seventies. Dressed in a striped floor-length dress and her silver hair pulled back in a tight bun, she had the look of an Italian grandmother who spent hours fussing over her sauces.

"Oh come *on*," Olivia cried, exasperated. "I

write about authentic culture, not this touristy nonsense." She shook her head. "I can't take this assignment. There's no way this ends as a positive for Sicily, not with this whole cookery thing going on too."

"Even better," Erica said eagerly. "Readers *love* negative reviews. Half the travel shows on TV now are about crusty expats irritated with their surroundings. If this thing is a crock of crap then expose it."

Olivia rolled her eyes, but Erica could see she was reconsidering. "Besides," she continued, "it's only five days. Kick butt on this, and we can send you wherever you want on your next assignment."

Olivia took a deep breath. She reminded herself that she was lucky—at twenty-nine, she had an incredibly enviable position and wasn't tethered to a desk. She knew she had to consider it.

"Can I think about it?" she asked.

"Take the night," Erica responded over the ring of the phone on her desk, "but I'm gonna need to know in the morning."

CHAPTER 2

*a*fterwards, Olivia pushed open the door to a coffee house up the street from the office.

She found the crowds of busy professionals oddly soothing—it helped her clear her head and think.

And she sure needed to think after that meeting. She ordered a black coffee and found a place at a bay window. She sat there for a few moments, sipping occasionally from her coffee.

Suddenly, she remembered the pamphlet Erica had given her. She pulled it from her back pocket and began reading.

THE FOOD OF LOVE
CHEF ISABELLA'S SICILIAN COOKING
CLASSES

Experience all that Taormina has to offer in this four-night, five-day culinary vacation.
Visitors have the chance to work with self-taught Sicilian chef Isabella Bottaro, whose work has been featured in countless cookery magazines and books all throughout Italy.
Spend your days exploring the enchanting Sicilian town of Taormina—its sprawling mountains, sloping hillsides, luxurious beaches, and classical Italian and Greek streets that bring out the best of Sicily.
Evenings at Isabella's Villa are spent feasting on authentic handmade Sicilian recipes specially picked to match the skill level and needs of students - beginners and experienced chefs alike.

"RIGHT," Olivia muttered under her breath, "even cheesier than I thought."

It read like the thousands of other tourist brochures she'd collected over her travels.

They all advertised "authentic cultural experiences" that usually turned out to be based on stereotypes rather than local flavour.

It was exactly this kind of cultural disintegration that she strove to combat in her writing.

Still, she'd promised Erica she'd give it a chance. She scanned the rest of the brochure.

ISABELLA'S PHILOSOPHY

*Experiencing the world begins at the dinner table. While it is easy to find "authentic" in any corner of the world, what makes Isabella's class different is the attention she gives to each and every student. Isabella believes that cooking is a personal experience meant to be lived and enjoyed in the moment. Whether the student comes with no experience or has professional training at top cookery schools in the world, Isabella will provide one-on-one guidance and insight. After all, as Isabella always says, "*Non c'è megghiu sarsa di la fami.*"*

ALWAYS ONE TO DO HER homework, Olivia pulled out her phone and entered the Italian phrase into her translation app.

"Hunger is the best sauce," it said.

That made her laugh; the phrase was pure kitsch—but it *had* elicited a response. It was sufficient at least, to make her start looking up travel site reviews of the cookery course.

All gave the Isabella's Villa high marks, most saying the same laudatory things. But then, she came across one in particular that caught her attention:

"MaryEllen87:

I'm not one to fall for touristy things like classes or tours, but my girlfriend insisted we take Isabella's cooking classes together on our trip to Sicily. I only agreed after looking at pictures of the grounds and the proximity to Mount Etna. However, when we arrived, I was instantly taken aback by the sheer beauty and warmth of the villa. Its stone walls shone brightly in the sunlight and glimmered in the moonlight. The patios became a place of refuge, a perfect setting to release all of our travel woes.

"But what really won me over was Isabella herself. I'm not a cook by any means. I prefer a hamburger over a fancy seafood dish. I was scep-

tical at what I could possibly learn in five days, but here I am, back in Chicago a month later, and I am still in love with cooking. Isabella made her "classes" accessible, and personable, and I left her villa feeling like I could conquer the world. I cannot thank her enough for it. This place and experience is not one to miss. See Taormina and meet Isabella. It will change your life."

"IT WILL CHANGE YOUR LIFE?" Olivia muttered. "Please."

But it was a challenge if ever she heard one.

As she finished her coffee, she began composing an email to Erica; she'd made her decision.

CHAPTER 3

*I*mpatiently tapping her heel on the linoleum floors, Kate O'Toole fidgeted listlessly in the plush chair of her doctor's office in Cork.

It had been at least fifteen minutes, but Dr. White still hadn't arrived to go over her test results. The wait was almost unbearable, and it didn't help that the chair next to her remained occupied.

Normally, Ed would have gone with her to these appointments. As they waited for the doctor to arrive, her husband would hold her hand gently, reminding her that everything would be okay, no matter what the doctor had to say.

But month after month, payment after payment, Ed's enthusiasm for the process had dwindled. And when it came time to make today's appointment, he'd opted out altogether, blaming a work issue he couldn't get out of and Kate had to get through it by herself.

At this stage, she should have been used to it. Infertility treatments had become just another part of her daily routine.

At the start of her cycle each month, they would visit the office for a consultation and a plan of action. She and Ed would quickly accept whatever the doctor had to suggest in terms of treatment.

Then, over about a month, she would subject herself to painful shots, horrid medications, and endless blood draws and ultrasounds.

All of that just to conceive a single baby.

It had been over a year since they had started the process. Before that, they had tried for five years to conceive naturally with no luck.

Now, at thirty-five, hope seemed to fade away faster with each passing day. These end-of-cycle appointments were just another opportunity to remind Kate of her age, her health, and her diminishing chances of ever holding her own child.

Doctor White gingerly knocked on his office door. Kate stood to greet him, shaking his hands heartily, hoping that he would glance her a smile, a wink, a nod—anything that would give her a hint that good news was about to come. But just like all the other appointments, the doctor had his nose in their paperwork, eyes remaining stuck on the large stack of documents.

"No Ed today?" His concern struck her as another sign that this appointment was not going to go as she had prayed.

"No. Work wouldn't let him off today. You know how that goes…" She couldn't bring herself to lie much more about the situation. How could she tell her doctor that her own husband had given up on their chances?

"That's a shame. We'll just have to talk the two of us, then." He looked back down at the paperwork, clearing his throat a bit as he seemingly searched for what to say next. With a burst of air, he let the news out, "I'm sorry, Kate, it's negative again. I'm afraid your body is just not responding to the medication and treatment plans."

Kate stared at him with a blank face. While in past appointments, she had allowed herself to show a hint of sadness, even cry, she was far past that now. She had heard Doctor White say the same thing for the last fourteen months, and at this point, she wasn't sure what an appropriate reaction would be. Instead of reacting with all the hurt and anger she had bottled up inside, she simply said, "Okay."

"I think we need to reevaluate the whole thing at this point. What we are doing at the moment is not working. And by the look of you and the fact that Ed isn't here, I think we all should take a break."

"A break?" That word frightened her. A break meant no trying, no medication, nothing. It meant time away from fighting this thing. And at this point, time meant the world in terms of conceiving a healthy child.

"Sometimes being in the right headspace is what you need to conceive. Stress and fatigue can take a huge toll on the body, let alone on a couple, and after six years of trying for a baby, you and Ed need a break. So I am giving it to you. Take the next month or two to get away, go on a holiday or something, and enjoy each other's company. You deserve it."

She wiped a few teardrops away from her eyes and focused on sounding as clinical as possible "Maybe," she said, "but there's got to be something else we can do. I'm just—"

"Kate," Doctor White said, smiling sadly and sympathetically, "I want to keep going. I really do. Seeing you deliver a beautiful baby would be amazing. But given where we are, I… I'm just afraid I can't continue working with you, at least not like this. All I'm asking is that you give it a month. Just one. And after that, we can start again."

With this, Doctor White stood up and turned towards his filing cabinet. He placed her manila folder into the metal organizer with the rest of the stack. Kate's heart thudded along with the sound of the drawer door slamming shut. She too stood, hastily saying her good-byes, and walked out the door of his office.

CHAPTER 4

*B*ack home, she headed straight for the bedroom at the top of the second floor, passing by the open doors of the empty rooms.

When Ed and Kate had purchased the place in the suburbs of Cork City nearly ten years ago, they had intended to fill the space with many children.

Now, the rooms were ghosts, occupied by office desks and guest beds. The rest of the house stood eerily silent as it always had.

Kate fell onto her bed, her head smothered into the pillows, waiting for tears to come. Instead, she found herself strangely restless and devoid of emotion, so she moved to the computer.

She started by looking up other fertility specialists in Ireland, but she quickly realized that switching doctors would likely mean starting this entire process over again. She couldn't put her marriage through that again— she couldn't put her*self* through that again.

And so, her mind wandered back to the doctor's office and that word: *holiday*. Because of the price of treatments and the pressure to be near her doctor, the couple hadn't ventured out of the country in years.

Maybe it was time for a break away from this empty house and the stuffy doctor's office. Maybe it would save her marriage from eroding even further.

She began a quick search online. Ed had always mentioned Italy as one of his dream destinations. If she was going to persuade him to go anywhere, picking a location that he wanted the most was probably her best bet. But prices for trips to Rome or Venice were astronomical. He would never agree to that.

Then, she came across Sicily. Looking at the average temperatures for the time of year, and the pictures of the beautiful sandy beaches, it seemed to have everything a couple could want. There was culture, art, beautiful scenery, nice hotels, etc. Compared to the rest of the Italian hot spots, a quick break there would be a steal.

Kate spent the rest of the afternoon researching the island of Sicily. She made spreadsheets of ideas and itineraries with prices and breakdowns. She included activities and sites she knew Ed wouldn't be able to resist. Her mind was flooded with thoughts of holding hands and strolling down stone piazzas while eating fresh gelato.

SHE WAS SO PREOCCUPIED with her activity, she didn't even hear the bedroom door open. Ed quietly snuck in, throwing his suit coat on the bed as he stripped off his tie and belt. Hearing the thud of his body hitting the edge of the bed, Kate turned to face her husband.

In his mid-thirties, he still looked just the same as the day she married him. His blonde hair was shorter, but he still had those baby blue eyes pinched by laugh lines. The only difference was he looked more tired now, almost defeated. Darker lines under his eyes became more puffy. The way he held his body was a bit more hunched and subdued.

"So what did the doctor say?" His face showed no sign of hope.

"He said we need a holiday." It came out a bit blunter than she'd intended, but she didn't regret it. Blunt might well be the best way to broach the subject.

"A holiday?" He stared at her quizzically, almost mocking her. She just gazed back at him with a tired expression. "No, seriously," he continued, "What did Doctor White say?"

"He said," she repeated with a sigh, "that we needed a holiday, Ed. He is not going to treat us next month. He recommended that we get away from everything."

"Are you joking?" His face contorted in annoyance. "We're paying that guy God knows how many thousands to tell us we need a damn holiday? We don't need a holi-day; what we *need* is a baby!" He placed his head in his hands, covering his eyes out of frustration. Kate stood up from the desk and sat next to him, rubbing her hand down the small of his back, undoing the top button of his shirt.

"Love, I think he's right. We need to get away from all this for a while. Being in this house all day, alone, with nothing to think about except the fact that I can't conceive is just adding stress and pressure. It's not good for my mind or my body. And it's not good for us."

He remained motionless, refusing to glance up from his hollowed palms, so she pressed on. "You have some holiday time saved up, and we could put together the money for something cheap and cheerful. I was thinking we could take that trip to Italy we've always talked about doing. The mainland's a little pricey, but if we stay in Sicily, hotels and food are working out fairly cheap. Think about it: we could go climb mountains, see Greek ruins, relax in the sun by a pool. Anything you want to do."

The two sat in silence, her attempting to comfort him while he bore deeper into despair.

Finally, he broke. "No, Kate, I can't."

"You can't... what, get the time off?" She had expected him to resist the idea, but he was so definitive.

"*This*, Kate," he said, looking directly into her large almond eyes, "I can't do *this*." His hand swept back a length of chestnut colored hair that had fallen from behind her ear.

She pulled away from him, tears stinging her eyes.

"Ed," she said, her voice wavering, "*I* have to go. I *have* to. I can't stay here another month just… *waiting*." Her voice pleaded with him to understand her. "And if you're not going to go with me, well then, I'll go on my own."

He stood up and shuffled to the dresser on the opposite side of the bed. Then he pulled out his wallet and tossed her a silver credit card.

"So go." With that, her husband opened the bedroom door, walked down the stairs, and turned on the television in the living room.

KATE GRASPED THE CARD, unsure of what to do next. She inhaled a shallow breath and went back to the desk. OK, if that's what he wanted, she would do it. She would go alone to Sicily. She was going to take a trip all for her. She wanted to sit on the beach, the ocean spray licking her feet. She wanted to walk up the side of a volcano and stare at the valleys below. She wanted to do everything that Sicily had to offer.

With that train of thought, Kate sat down at her computer and brought up the list of options she'd been searching through earlier.

CHAPTER 5

*a*fter an eight-hour flight from Toronto, Martha Walters was relieved to finally have her feet on the ground.

She was never one for travel.

And despite flying at least twice a year to visit her children across the United States, she still couldn't breathe right until she had safely made it out of the terminal.

Today's flight marked the longest trip she had ever taken, and that return of breath was more heavenly than ever.

The relief was short-lived when she regained her bearings. This wasn't just another airport in the States.

Leonardo Da Vinci Airport was packed

with tourists speaking every foreign language imaginable while gesturing towards signs written in Italian.

To Martha, it might as well have been hieroglyphics. She sat down on a metal bench and started scanning her translation book in an attempt to figure out how to find her connecting flight from Rome to Palermo.

A man in a dusty brown suit sat next to her tying his leather loafers. She knew that she would have to be brave.

"Sir? Pardon me. Sir?" She tapped his shoulder gently, unsure of what the cultural protocol was here. He glanced up at her, his greying mustache twitching in annoyance. "English? Do you speak English?"

He lifted his hands and gestured a clear no. She glanced back to her translation book where the phrases were. She started slowly,

"Dov'è terminal due?" He looked at her and smiled. Pointing his tanned finger upwards and to the left, he motioned towards a large lit-up sign with arrows pointing in the direction.

Relieved, she smiled and stood quickly. As she walked away, she shouted towards the gentleman "Grazie, Grazie." He watched her petite frame go off on a small sprint towards the direction of the arrows.

TERMINAL 2 LOOKED JUST like the rest of the airport she had come through. Lofty with large white beams over her head, the space reminded Martha of the airport hangers her husband worked in years ago. She had wished William was here with her today. He would have loved this adventure.

When her children had presented her with the airline tickets to Sicily and the brochure for a cookery holiday in Taormina, it took all that she had not to break down at the thought of going alone.

She had been a widow for five years now. William had passed away suddenly, without little warning. The loss was crushing, but Martha had powered through knowing that her children needed her to be strong. They needed a mother and a father, and she would be tasked with playing both roles.

However, reality hit her fast. Only a couple of years after William's death, her children began leaving the nest. And worse, leaving

Canada. The twins, Julia and Jennifer went down to college in Boston first. A year later, Christopher followed in his father's footsteps and enlisted in the Air Force. April was married nearly three years ago and now lived in California.

For the last two years, the large brick bungalow in the suburbs was shared by only Martha and her youngest son, Kurt.

However, just last week, she said goodbye to her baby as he unpacked boxes and rearranged his college dorm room, his new home for the foreseeable future.

She was no longer a mother - or at least, it wasn't her primary job anymore. She had taken up classes and spent hours volunteering, but her children grew concerned when Martha lost her lustre for life.

Things that had interested her previously, such as church or playing her violin, had suddenly gone stale. Most nights were spent watching television or writing emails to her children in hopes they would reply quickly.

And now, she was here alone, overwhelmed and culture-shocked at the thought of being in Europe.

Her children had intended for this to be a life-changing experience. "You get to go somewhere new, see the world, and learn how to cook a real Italian meal!" they'd insisted enthusiastically while presenting her with a new set of luggage filled to the brim with glossy pictures of Sicily's coastline. The twins had even gone to the trouble of calling the community centre Martha volunteered at to arrange her days off.

And that night, Kurt led the group as they sang "Happy Birthday" to her in Italian, as she blew out the fifty candles affixed to a cannoli cake April had made.

But the truth was, Martha hadn't wanted any of this. At her age, travel was out of the question. Just lugging around suitcases in the airport was enough of a chore, let alone attempting to get to grips with Italian or figure out menu options. If she wanted a beach, she could have gone to Florida. And if she wanted to learn how to cook, there were plenty of cooking shows on TV or books in the store. Italy just seemed like a waste—a way to get her to leave home and stop hounding the kids, probably.

Martha took out her cell phone and turned the WIFI signal back on. Searching her email inbox, she had hoped to see something from her children. Instead, it was as empty as usual.

She drafted a short, cheerful group email letting them know she had arrived in Rome safely, and that she had another twenty minutes until her plane to Palermo boarded. She promised to call one of them when she reached Taormina in the afternoon.

Glancing around the gate, she saw she wasn't the only one with her head in a cell phone or computer. Directly seated across from her, a woman in her late twenties was also busy typing away at a laptop.

Her dark brown, pin-straight hair fell into her face as she looked furiously at the screen. When she was done, she dramatically closed the laptop and tossed it into her leather bag. Seemingly exasperated, she sat back with her arms crossed tightly across her chest, muttering to herself in English, and what Martha was sure was an American accent.

Noticing Martha staring, the woman put on a quick, almost guilty smile, obviously embarrassed by her display of irritation. Martha's motherly instincts kicked in immediately. "I know the feeling," she said with a little laugh. "But we must remember that it is still only midnight or so back home"

"Yeah, I guess you're right." Olivia glanced back at her open bag and then again at the woman seated next to her. Not unused to striking up conversations in airports, she turned back to the woman who she guessed was not US-born but Canadian, "Are you headed to Palermo too?"

"Yes, but then I have to take a bus to a place called Taormina. I'm there for a cooking retreat—a gift from my children. How about you?"

Olivia beamed curiously at the coincidence. "I'm also heading to Taormina. My editor set me up to review a cooking class believe it or not. Is yours the one taught by Chef Isabella?" The woman smiled and nodded. "Olivia Bennett. I write for *The Wanderer* magazine." She stretched out an arm towards her companion.

"Martha Walters, just a mom. That's why I'm here actually. My children, for some reason, conspired to get me out of the house and off to an entirely different continent." She blushed slightly at her honesty.

"You don't sound too excited to be in Italy. Is it your first time?"

"Yes. My late husband had always wanted to go to Europe, but we never got the chance while raising five children. I never really had much interest. I'd rather be back home in Canada. I'm not one for travel."

"To be honest, I'm not too keen on this trip either. Sicily was on my do-not-travel list, but my publisher went nuts over Taormina and this cookery vacation, so it was either go check it out or find a new job. Luckily for us, it's only a few days, right?"

"Right." Martha smiled, thankful to be in the company of someone much more secure about the situation than she was. The two continued chatting, Martha transfixed by Olivia's stories on the road, and the places she had travelled over the years.

For Olivia's part, she was glad to find someone to chat to, and especially happy to have met a fellow culinary student.

She was used to being alone and independent it was kinda of refreshing to just chat with a fellow traveller and share the experience. Perhaps this whole Sicily thing would be a change of pace?

Already she got the feeling that this trip would certainly be different.

CHAPTER 6

*S*icily was as gorgeous as Kate had imagined it.

The sun-drenched, cramped streets opened up to an expansive blue-green bay, and the low-lying stone buildings reminded her of what she had envisioned for the settings of fantasy stories of her youth.

The island was a mixture of Greek, Arabic, and Italian classical architecture, and wandering the pavements of Palermo, she wanted nothing more but to open one of the many red and brown doors and step into a Sicilian resident's life.

She only had a couple of hours to explore the place before the next bus left for Taormina, the beautiful hilltop town set high above the sea, where the cookery holiday she'd booked was located.

Unsure of where to start, she had her cab driver leave her at the Piazza Pretoria and instantly, she spotted the iconic Fontana della Vergogna. It was striking with its nude figures bursting out of the low-lying pools of water. Certainly, it was not something you'd see every day back home in Cork.

Taking a seat on the steps leading up to the fountain, Kate pulled her small suitcase and backpack towards her. She watched as Italian women in their large, floppy hats and flowing earth-toned skirts passed her by. Even the men seemed effortlessly chic in their pale-coloured suits and small-lensed sunglasses. All breezily unaware of the raw, unique beauty they were a part of.

She breathed it all in; the sea air, the warmth of the Mediterranean sun, the delicious scents coming from the local restaurants. She allowed herself to lean back and take a moment to release her thoughts and fears. For just a moment, Kate didn't have to focus on the baby she didn't have or the equally absent husband. This moment was just for her alone.

But in the back of her mind, there was one thing she couldn't let go: Ed.

She wanted him here, next to her, so that she could lean her head on his shoulder and talk about her desire to look so effortless as the Palermo women. She wanted someone to stroll the Italian streets with, point out the beautiful scenery and discuss what they might eat at lunch.

Hearing his voice would surely bring him here to her in spirit, even if it was just for a couple of minutes. She grabbed for her phone, searching for her husband's name in her list of contacts. She held her breath while she listened to the phone ring on the other end. She was almost giddy with excitement at all the things she wanted to share with him. A smile grew wide on her face as the familiar, soothing voice of her husband answered.

"Ed," she gushed. "Guess where I am right now, at this very second?" She listened closely to the sounds on the other end. She could hear voices, voices other than her husband's.

"Can I call you back?" Ed said then. "I'm, ah, a bit busy right now."

Disbelief overcame her.

"Excuse me? Ed? Where are you? Why do I hear in the background? Aren't you supposed to be at work?" A million questions washed over her. She couldn't understand why Ed would just forget about her so suddenly without another thought. He didn't even care enough to check if she was safe, or actually in Sicily.

For all he knew, she could be in China wandering along the Great Wall.

"It's just the … television you hear. Everything's grand. But I'll have to call you back." With that, she heard a click, and the sound on the other end went from flooded with sound and movement, to nothingness.

Kate wasn't sure what to feel. She angrily tossed the phone into her bag. Sitting in this spot, with the happy tourists passing her by, she began to feel light-headed and sick. She needed to get away. She needed some sustenance.

nsure of exactly where she was heading, she turned right past an ancient cathedral near the fountain.

The winding streets became a maze of curves and crisscrosses as she passed through corridor after corridor.

Stores and shops buzzed with commerce. Outdoor vendors set up shop with all kinds of wares: flowers, newspapers, seafood stands, and gelato. The smell of briny winds grew nearer, indicating that she was nearing the bay. *Thank goodness*, she thought to herself.

As she rounded the next bend, her stomach rumbled audibly; she needed something to eat.

With only an hour or so to spare before the bus left, it would have to be a quick bite, but she was not allowing herself to skimp out on quality or experience. She planned to stop at the first restaurant with an outdoor patio to get the true Palermo experience.

Rounding a stone corner, she stumbled into the outdoor seating area of a pretty little cafe. She glanced around nervously looking for an English menu, but with no luck, she took her seat at the very back of the patio and put a menu to her face. She took out her phone once again and this time pulled up her translation app, quickly looking up menu items.

Two tables away, a young man of about late twenties, in a white button-down shirt, watched Kate intently, smiling at her panicked expression. He stroked his stubbly beard, debating if he should take pity on the poor foreigner. Subtly, he took his cappuccino and napkin and moved to the table next to her.

"Pardon me." His accent was thick but gentle. It had hints of humour in it. "Do you need help ordering?"

Kate barely registered the younger guy now

sitting less than ten feet from her. "Oh. No, thank you. I'm grand."

Just as she was about to turn away, a female waitress approached. She spoke quickly in Italian as Kate nervously looked away. She was sure she had asked her what she wanted to drink, so Kate responded by pointing to a random wine on the wine list. The waitress chuckled a little and repeated what she said again slowly and deliberately. Kate again held up her menu and pointed a finger at the same wine.

The woman held up her hands and firmly said, "No. No today." Kate pointed to another wine on the list and looked up at the dark-skinned Italian with hopeful eyes. The woman shook her head furiously. Reaching over, she flipped the large food menu to the back page and pointed annoyed, at the bottom selections. Kate still could not comprehend what was going on.

The man next to her again leaned over. She is saying that those wines are not for this afternoon. Those are dinner wines. You must order a lunch wine."

"Oh. Really?" Kate felt flushed as she realized what a fool she must look: just another ignorant tourist.

The man continued, "Would you allow me?" She nodded and he began to speak to the waitress, who scribbled furiously on her pad as he ordered. When he finished, she smiled brightly at him, ignoring Kate altogether, and headed back inside.

"So, what did you order?"

"A white table wine to start," he winked, "and a glass of flat water. For food, I started you off with an octopus salad and then ordered my favourite meal, the caponata. It's an aubergine stew. If you're sharing, I may even order you dessert."

Despite his forwardness, Kate smiled. The guy was certainly blunt and outgoing, but she liked how friendly and charming he was too. She agreed to share a dessert with him if he ordered her something with chocolate, her ultimate indulgence.

The wine and octopus salad came out quickly, and immediately, the mouthwatering combination of olive oil, lemon, and oregano melted away Kate's residual anger towards Ed. Without a care in the world, she tore into the plate, devouring each oily and lemon-zested morsel. The juices trickled down her chin carelessly, freely. She didn't even dare to use a napkin for fear of losing another taste.

As she cleared her plate, she turned back towards the man. "Thank you so much. That was... I don't even know. I don't think *delicious* would describe it accurately."

He laughed and outstretched his long arm to her.

"Marco, and I am glad that you enjoyed it."

"Kate. It is great to meet you."

"Ah," he said, clapping his hands together, "Like the English princess!" She blushed slightly as he continued. "So, what brings you here to Palermo, *Principessa* Kate?"

She beamed back at him. "Just passing through," she said. "I'm actually supposed to be moving on in about," she checked her watch, "about thirty minutes, actually. Heading to Taormina."

"Taormina? Really? I am headed there as well. My business is there. I am just in Palermo to check on some family. Are you taking the 2:30 bus?"

"Yes, that was my plan. I need to be at my

accommodation by five." She was leery about giving this stranger more detail. Yet, everything in her said he could be trusted, that he was relatively harmless. Still, she knew that as a solo female traveller, she had to be a bit more aware and less 'chatty Irish'.

"Well, if you would like a guide, I would be happy to accompany you to the bus stop. It isn't far from here, but it can be tricky to find if you only have a tiny tourist map on hand." He gestured to the wrinkled mess of a map sticking out from her carry-on bag. Again, she blushed, embarrassed by just how obvious it was that she was a tourist. She couldn't even pass for an experienced traveller.

Still, before she could agree to him joining her, she felt she needed to make it clear to this guy that she was married. After all, she didn't exactly know what his intentions were...

"That would be great, thank you. But before we go, I need to call my husband back home. I like to tell him when I plan on boarding foreign buses with strange men." She laughed at herself, trying to lighten the mood.

To her surprise, Marco responded with an equally jovial laugh. "Ah, I know you Americans think us Italian men are only about one thing, but I can assure you that I am just in it for the conversation and potential dessert." He winked at her, and his accompanying smile gave him a sly fox appearance, just as she had imagined flirty Italian men to be.

CHAPTER 8

The two enjoyed the rest of their meal, each keeping to their own table.

Kate found the stew to be almost as delicious as the octopus salad. Fresh and juicy, it was the right mixture of hearty and comforting without being overwhelming. And as she promised, the two enjoyed dessert, a shared chocolate tart.

When the time came to catch their bus, she realized how thankful she was for Marco's help. The cobblestone Palermo streets were a massive spider web, yet Marco navigated them effortlessly.

He bypassed the heavily travelled areas

while managing to skim minutes off of their would-be journey time with shortcuts and alleyways.

The whole way, he still managed to play tour guide, pointing out the most interesting points along the way: a bookshop that only sold antique texts in Latin, a record store frequented by the hippest Palermo citizens, the entrance to a palace, the top of the Greek theatre popping up from behind a building.

The bus stop itself was the least impressive sight. Attached to the train station, it was as dreary as any back home in Ireland. As the bus wasn't any more luxurious or exciting, Kate secretly lamented the end of her Palermo adventure.

The first stop was Catania, another coastal town equal in charm as it was to views. Marco pointed out the looming Mt. Etna, describing it as the centre of all Sicilians' world. A volcano that contained all of the famous Italian tempers.

When boarding the bus, she and Marco had taken a seat across from two women travelling together. One with slightly greying hair and a dishevelled look, and the other a slick twenty-something who looked as stylish and effortlessly chic as the other Italian women on the bus. The two chatted animatedly in English about their journey and Kate quickly deduced from their accents that they were American.

After a little while, Marco, sitting on the outside seat, interjected himself into the women's conversation.

"*Buongiorno*, ladies! I am sorry to interrupt, but are you headed to Taormina also?" He oozed charm, and he knew it, Kate thought chuckling to herself.

The older woman ignored him, evidently more off-put than Kate had been by this Italian stranger's insistence to strike up a conversation. The younger woman, however, happily replied. "Yes, yes we are. We are on our way to Villa Isabella."

"Villa Isabella?" Kate perked up. "That's where I'm headed too."

"Yes, we're there for the cookery class. Are you as well?" The older woman now seemed just as enthused to meet a fellow student as Kate was.

She nodded, "I am. I hear it is amazing. I'm not much of a cook, but I suppose there's no better place to learn Italian cooking than Italy itself." She grinned, hoping their response would be equally enthusiastic. "I'm Kate."

"Great to meet you. I'm Martha, and this is Olivia. Olivia is a travel writer. We met on the connecting plane from Ro—"

The information was enough for Marco to pounce, "Olivia. What a beautiful name! Almost as beautiful as mine, Marco. Tell me, how long will you stay in Italy, Olivia? And is your trip for business or pleasure?"

Olivia took it all in her stride. It was easy to see that out of the three women, she was the most experienced in dealing with flirtatious foreigners. "Just here for the cookery break. That's my assignment."

"What a shame to call Italy an 'assignment.' Italy is life... it is art... it is love! There is no country like it." Marco gestured wildly, his arms dramatic yet inviting.

"I'm sure I could argue that," muttered Olivia in reply. She smiled at the other women. "But we'll all have to decide for ourselves."

Marco laughed and continued to argue, trying to keep his conversation just between him and Olivia. Kate watched patiently, noticing Martha behave almost like a protective mother hen, ensuring that her younger companion was not getting in too deep with this stranger.

As the bus edged slowly up the hill on the zig-zag roadways leading to Taormina, finally coming to a stop near the centre of the town, Marco helped the women gather their bags from the overhead storage.

Ever the gentleman, he kissed each of their hands as the three loaded into a taxi bound for Villa Isabella.

Before the driver could take off, he peeked in "Before I let you leave, I have to ask... what did you bring to give to Chef Isabella? It is rude to go to a Sicilian's home without a gift of some sort."

"Oh, I didn't bring anything!" Martha and Olivia nodded in agreement to Kate's reply. "Should we pick something up on the way, maybe a bottle of wine?"

"No!" he exclaimed, almost offended. "It is even worse to bring a bottle of wine to a Sicilian's home."

"Why so? In the US, it's almost customary."

Olivia was intrigued, taking out a notepad to jot down his reply.

"It is akin to saying that your host does not have good taste in wine. In Sicily, we grow up knowing what wines are the best and what are not so good. Plus, as a chef, your host will already have wines paired with the meals."

The three women sat in silent contemplation. This sudden injection of cultural mores was both valuable and telling.

"What I suggest you do is bring her flowers," Marco went on. "It's not the best, but good for when you meet a stranger for the first time. I'll have the driver bring you to a shop a street down from the villa." Without giving the women time to interject, he began speaking in Italian to the driver, both nodding in agreement.

"Ciao, till later. I'm sure I shall see you around." With his hands in his pocket, Marco let go of the open window and watched as the car sped off towards Villa Isabella.

CHAPTER 9

The taxi curved up the winding driveway to the entrance of Villa Isabella. Peppered with lush, leafy olive trees and bushes, and bordered by tall Italian pines, the terracotta yellow mansion shone as brightly as the sun.

While Olivia had checked out the estate online before departing, the sight of the home in person was enough to take her breath away. Her jaded facade slowly melted away as she spotted the clear blue pool jettisoning out of the landscape, and the expansive patio overlooking the scene.

This alone was worth the visit ...

Standing by the brown wooden door was whom Olivia quickly identified as Chef Isabella. The woman's black and white pinstriped dress engulfed her petite, yet stout body. Her silver and black hair was knotted in a loose braid that dripped over her collarbone. She fit right in with the Italian Renaissance scene.

The women disembarked, each slowly approaching their host with gentle caution. Olivia gingerly carried the bundle of sunflowers they had picked out from the flower shop Marco had directed them to.

"*Che meraviglia*! You all arrive together! The fates must have been on our sides today." Isabella smiled brightly at the group, as she outstretched her arms first to Martha, embracing her in a large hug and exchanging gentle cheek kisses. Kate was next, but instead of a hug, Isabella grasped her hands tenderly.

Olivia, flowers in arms, was never one for affection. Even though she was worldly and had grown accustomed to the traditional European greeting, she still shied away. For some reason, Isabella seemed to sense this, and instead took the flowers from her and gently touched her cheek with the soft, wrinkled palm of her hand.

"*Grazie*, my dear. *Grazie*. These are beautiful." Isabella deeply inhaled the scent of the sunflowers, genuinely impressed by the gesture.

"The flowers are from all of us." Olivia went down the line, introducing each of the other women. "We wanted to thank you for welcoming us to your beautiful home. It is breathtaking."

"Well, you must see inside first before you say that." With a quick turn on her low-heeled leather shoes, Isabella opened the large wooden doors and walked inside with a motion for the women to follow.

All three silently took the cue, grabbed their bags, and rushed to catch up with the sprite Sicilian.

"These are the bedrooms. Each of you has single rooms, but you will all need to share the two bathrooms on this floor. My room is downstairs, near the *Cucina*, the kitchen. I like to sleep where the action is." She grinned as Kate giggled.

Isabella glanced at a dangling gold pocket

watch that hung from her dress. "*Accidenti*! We only have a couple of hours till the market closes. Unpack quickly and meet me downstairs in the living quarters. We have lots to do if we are to get dinner on the table by eight."

Olivia walked into the room closest to her. Alabaster walls and white linens dominated the speckled bedroom. Even the furniture was painted in an antique pale yellow that fit right into the scene.

Stark white, translucent thread curtains floated softly in the air, as a soft breeze pushed from the open window.

Setting her suitcase on the chair, she pushed back the drapery further and fully opened the shuttered window.

She let out a gasp as all of Taormina came into view. The villa itself sat on the lofty hillside, with the town itself sparkling right below her.

To the right was Mount Etna, the volcano. Straight ahead was the sea, dominating the landscape, its turquoise colour glimmering in the fading sun.

The rest of Sicily circled, forming a classic U-shape that gave Olivia the impression of being so close, yet so far away from civilization.

EAGER TO SEE the rest of the property, Olivia joined the other women and Isabella on the bottom level of the villa. The living room was expansive and also decked out in all-white. However, colourful accents like the red throw cushions or the yellow woven rug popped out from the scene.

Connected was the massive kitchen which Olivia instantly identified as a chef's paradise.

The white and tan workstations were decked out into five designated areas. Each had its own stove, oven, and sink along with an apron hanging from the counter drawer. Simple cooking utensils were tucked away in a decorative metal pot. In the corner of the room was a hanging display of pots, pans, lids, and cutlery hung on hooks and magnetic strips.

Isabella sat on a wooden stool at the centre station, furiously writing on brown parchment cards. She only took a moment to acknowledge the three women as they entered the space, speaking as she continued to write. "Welcome to the kitchen! Each of you has a workspace along with your apron. Two hours before breakfast and dinner, we will gather here. I will hand you a recipe card outlining what you will make, and then walk you individually through what to do. Normally, I would get to know you all a bit better first, so I will simply guess at your skill levels tonight.

"Each of my classes is different. I never pick the same recipe. What fun would that be for me? Tonight, I am thinking we'll start with some of my favourite recipes. Martha, you shall make the *antipasti*, the appetizer, *melanzane alla parmigiana*. Kate will make the *primo*, the first course. It is typically pasta, so I say we try *linguine al limone*. Olivia will make the *secondi*, the *Fettine alla Pizzaiola*. And I will make the dessert."

As their tutor assigned each student their mission for the evening, she handed out three cards with a recipe written in English.

Olivia studied her small stack, each card crunched with specific instructions and notes. Her own recipe didn't appear quite intimidating as the others. It was a simple meat and tomato sauce dish. However, she was relieved that her cooking skills wouldn't necessarily be put to the test just yet.

"In Sicily, eating isn't just a thing we *do.*" Isabella went on. "We say *sperimentiamo*: we *experience* it. To make a good Sicilian meal, you must know the basics before you become a master. I do not expect you to walk out of here in four days as authentic Italian chefs. Instead, I expect you all to learn about what it means to be an *artista*. To do so, you must know that there are rules when it comes to eating here." She emphasized the world 'rule' as if it was something they should take heed of, like a law or a commandment. Olivia rummaged in her bag for her notepad, hoping to take all the wisdom she could get for her article.

"Your first rule is that not everything is in season. I have been to America, and I have seen your giant markets with your fruits and vegetables lined up on display. That is no good, to have so many options at all times. The best in life is what is available now, what is *fresco*. There should be no worry about the future or the past. In Italy we say, *Ciò che conta è oggi*— what matters is today. We work with what God has given us, not with what we wish we had. So when we plan our meals, we plan with the season in mind."

Olivia scribbled away furiously as Martha continued to stare at her card. Kate, on the other hand, looked directly at Isabella with a quizzical look on her face. Her eyes widened with each bit of wisdom.

"Before we get started, we obviously need ingredients. So we will go to Taormina's best shops and markets before they close. I will show you how to shop for what you truly need."

CHAPTER 10

The three women duly followed Isabella out of the kitchen and down the stone steps that jutted out from the hillside.

The actual town was about a ten-minute walk straight down the steps to reach the centre. The stone steps changed quickly into light and grey checkerboard pavement, and the streets soon became overrun with tourists from cruise ships and nearby hotels. Yet Isabella took everything in her stride, seamlessly pushing through the crowds, with her students following closely behind.

Most of the market's vendors and shops were located along Porta Catania. Lined up with their colourful fruits and produce on tables, and the beds of trucks, the owners of the mobile stalls shouted at their customers and other proprietors.

As they stood at the foot of the market, all three women looked at each other and shuddered. Shopping here would not be as easy as it was in supermarkets, Isabella was right about that.

The chef turned towards her group before starting, "I have made a list of the ingredients we need for *la cena* tonight, as well as breakfast tomorrow morning. We'll start first with vegetables and then work our way to the outside for the meats and seafood. Always get last the things that will smell. Plus, meat vendors are more desperate to sell than the produce men."

She handed each a copy of the list. With only about ten items, it did not seem like it would take too long—just a quick shopping trip.

However, Martha quickly realized she had misjudged the task. Isabella insisted on stopping at each vegetable and fruit stall to squeeze, smell, and inspect each item. She would hold up an onion or a tomato and loudly point out the imperfections, much to the ire of the cart's owner. The women, stunned by her boldness and her ease of spotting rot or ripeness, nodded in silence.

About twenty stalls were ventured through when Isabella went to the end of the staircase street. "So, *miei cari*, who can tell me where we should get the best tomato from?"

Kate and Martha averted their eyes, obviously stumped by the question. Olivia chimed in confidently, "Nowhere. None of those vendors had a perfect vegetable or fruit."

Isabella placed her hand on her chin, studying the words as Olivia said them. "Let me ask you this: is life ever perfect? Have you ever found the juiciest peach or the ripest tomato? Have your beans ever been the most green that you've ever seen them?"

Olivia shook her head in reply, duly chastened.

"So, why should we look for perfection? None of these vendors will have it here. But even the dullest pea can taste as good as the next. A tomato with a bruise can still be as flavorful as before. Instead of searching for something that doesn't exist, we seek out what we think - in our hearts - is the best of what is presented to us."

With their heads held a bit higher, the women went back into the heart of the market-place, again stopping at each stall. Kate decided on the onions while Martha hunted down the beans. Olivia cautiously selected the peppers, unsure of what Isabella could mean by 'best of what is presented to us.'

When they were sure of their choices, Isabella would approve of the selection and then haggle with the vendor loudly in Italian. Each of the burly, sweaty men would at first appear off-put by Isabella's boldness and her instance at getting in the final word. When they would not relent, she would walk away to the vendor next to them, cooly passing them off until the owner would run towards her with a counteroffer.

The meat was an easier adventure. With only beef on the menu, they glided effortlessly past the men with meat on a spit, or hoisted on the top of a tent, to a small building in the corner of the market.

Inside, a balding man with a handlebar moustache greeted Isabella enthusiastically.

"The best way to buy your bigger items," Isabella said as she turned from the butcher back to her group, "is to find the person you trust the most. Federico has been selling me my beef for thirty-five years. I know that when I need the best of the best, Rico will provide."

The man returned with a package wrapped in red string and brown paper.

He kissed Isabella on the cheek and waved goodbye to the women as they marched back to the villa with their marketplace wares in paper sacks.

ONCE THEY SETTLED BACK IN, Isabella showed each student to their station. Olivia took her place at the one nearest the window. She donned her red apron and white chef's hat as she shook the tension and nervousness from her hands. As a traveller without a constant base, she rarely prepared for anyone, let alone had a home-cooked meal. The thought of cooking for three other women, one a professional chef, scared her senseless. Yet, she powered through, following Isabella's delicately written instructions word for word.

As she began to mix the sauce with the meat, Isabella appeared behind her shoulder, startling her. Previously, she had been keenly focused on Kate, who was struggling to find the right balance of lemon zest for her linguine. Now it was Olivia's turn to be in the pressure spot.

"You seem nervous, *mio bambino*. You shouldn't be. Even if you ruin the recipe, the trick about hosting with a group of friends and loved ones is that we care enough to lie to you." She smiled at her own joke as she placed her hands upon Olivia's shoulders, squeezing the tension away. "But let's try a taste anyway. Sampling is the best part of being a chef." She grabbed a large fork from the metal utensil pot and tasted a bit of the meat.

"Slightly overcooked, but still delicious. Try a bit."

Olivia took a bite herself as the tomato sauce she created burst into her mouth, the hearty beef texture following second, and the onion leaving a gentle kick.

"It's good, but I still overcooked it. It should be more tender, right?"

"Yes, it should. But it is as I said in the market: sometimes, even the food with imperfections can taste as good. No point in searching constantly for 'perfect' or 'best.'"

Olivia looked back down at her pan both messy, yet a work of art. Using her phone, she snapped a picture and debated who to send it to.

She could upload it on her social media pages where her followers could find it. But this felt like something so personal, something she wanted to share with those she cared for deeply. However, there was no one in Olivia's life worth this intimate accomplishment, she realised sadly.

Instead, she tucked the phone back into her pocket and began plating her food. Tonight, she wouldn't think about what was truly on her mind.

Instead, she would join the rest of the class as they feasted on their dinner at the table overlooking the crystal, navy blue sea.

CHAPTER 11

*T*he cell phone vibrated incessantly, shaking the antique bedside table until it rattled itself off the shelf and onto the wooden floor. It kept buzzing, the constant "zzz" "zzz" "zzz" echoing off the floorboards until Martha could take it no longer.

Rolling over, she grabbed in the dark for her pair of black reading glasses, knocking over a book in the process. She finally found the lamp switch and, the room now illuminated, found her phone still vibrating. Looking at the caller ID, she cursed mildly and answered the call.

"Kurt!" she hissed into the receiver, praying that the ruckus she was making in her room hadn't woken anyone else in the villa. "Do you know what time it is here? It's—" she held the phone away from her ear and checked the time "—four in the morning!"

"Mom." The voice on the other end was flat and even, and Martha's anger melted. Kurt, her youngest, always had a way of twisting her emotions around with just that pleading sound of his voice. "Something's happened. I need help."

She quickly sat up, brushing her hair wildly from her eyes. "What's wrong? Talk to me. I'm awake now." Her coddling voice was almost too eager.

"It's school. I, uh, got caught…" he waited for her to catch on. Martha's silence begged for more, "I was at this freshman party and there was beer …I didn't know any better."

Martha swallowed and attempted a tone that could be lecturing without coming off as angry. She only partly pulled it off.

"Kurt," she said in a measured tone, "you knew that was against school policy. You're still underage. I warned you about this." She listened as he murmured incoherently into the phone. Obviously, the matter was much more urgent than she had previously thought. "So, what does the school want to do about it?"

"They're suspending me!" he wailed, his usual emotional control failing. "What am I going to do? They want me to move out in three days. I can't move out in three days! And what about my classes? What about my major? I'm not going to be able to graduate on time. I'm not going to be able to pledge this year, Mom. What if they don't let me back?"

"Honey, slow down. Everything will work out. I will call later today when the school opens. I'll get this sorted out for you. For right now, just hang tight and stick to your room. Okay?" Her motherly instincts had kicked into high gear.

"Yeah, okay. You promise you'll call, Mom?" Her youngest sounded just like he did as a child: vulnerable and afraid.

"Yes. Now, I need to go back to sleep. The sun hasn't even come up yet in Italy. I love you." With that, Martha hung up the phone. A smile popped on her face.

For the first time in ages, she felt needed again.

CHAPTER 12

$\mathcal{K}$ate woke to birds singing outside her window. Early morning sunlight drenched her white room, giving it an almost ethereal appearance.

The entire scene looked as charming as she had envisioned it when she first decided to go on this trip. Stretching out her arms, she instinctively looked for her phone first.

No missed calls.

Getting up, she grabbed her robe, a towel, and her travel bag of toiletries. As she opened the door to head to the communal bathroom, she stopped short.

Outside her room sat a large floral bouquet

full of large yellow sunflowers, not too dissimilar to the ones they'd brought Isabella yesterday. But as their host had arranged these in a vase in the hallway she knew these were different.

Probably Isabella's way of returning the gesture.

She grabbed the bouquet, unsure what to do with it, and glanced at Olivia's and Martha's doors. Not seeing any matching bouquets, she assumed they were up and about and had already collected theirs.

She placed the flowers on her bedside locker and inhaled their earthy, succulent scent. It had been years since she had got flowers.

She had always insisted to Ed that it was a cliched, overpriced gesture, but the truth was, she was slightly envious of other women whose husbands went out of their way to pick up flowers for birthdays or special occasions.

The dissatisfied thought caught her attention instantly, and she shook her head wildly as a way to remove her from the moment. Today was not about her disappointments.

Today was about her, her relaxation, and her quest to learn Italian cooking. With determination, Kate grabbed her towel and went to get ready for the breakfast lesson.

Once showered and dressed, she joined Olivia and Martha in the kitchen. Isabella was already busy preparing the ingredients and mixing bowls. However, it seemed the foursome wasn't alone this morning.

Kate was surprised to see Marco, their helpful stranger from yesterday, standing right in the kitchen alongside Isabella, chatting rapidly in Italian.

"Ah! Our *traversina* has arrived, and just in time." Isabella's attention whipped from Marco and onto a bashful Kate. "Come join us. And meet *mio nipote*, my grandson, Marco. We're learning how to make briosce to go with our morning gelato."

Grandson?

"Gelato?" Olivia chimed, seemingly more intrigued by the idea of dessert for breakfast, than Marco turning out to be a relative of their host.

Marco looked at her pointedly. "*Si*, gelato.

We sometimes have our pastries with shaved ice, but today, I brought gelato as a celebration of my triumphant return to Taormina." He winked at her and smiled.

Martha laughed heartily, "Wait until I tell my Kurt about dessert for breakfast!"

The three women gathered around Isabella's station as she began mixing flour, egg, milk, sugar, and butter into a giant jewel-coloured mixing bowl. "Most chefs are lazy," she sighed. "They buy their breakfast from shops or cafés. But the best breakfasts are the ones you make yourself."

The women mimicked her actions as they formed balls of dough in their white powdered hands.

Marco joined in, more confidently than the women, placing himself shoulder to shoulder with Olivia.

"Keep your flour to yourself, please," she said to him as he lightly tossed a handful of flour onto the top of her kneaded dough. Cupping her hands around some flour of her own, she blew the remains into his hair.

"I look like my grandmother now." He

turned and brushed it away, grinning over at Olivia as she continued to mould her briosce.

TWO HOURS LATER, the briosce was taken out of the oven as the students gathered their trays, each admiring their handiwork.

"In all my life, I've never made my own bread without a mixer." Martha looked down at her golden brown pastries with newfound pride as they moved to the wooden communal dining table.

Marco followed the group with a large, clear plastic tub of glossy, creamy gelato. He served Isabella first as she cut lightly into the centre of the pastry. Marco placed a dollop of the coffee-flavoured cold treat in the centre of the bun.

Kate and Martha seemed unsure of how to approach such a strange, rich breakfast. But Olivia, being the adventurer she was, jumped in headfirst, taking a large bite.

The sweet and eggy taste overwhelmed her senses, bringing back memories of childhood treats and simple, country meals. It was heavenly. The other two joined in, each having a similar reaction. All almost too overwhelmed to speak.

"The reward of a good meal is sometimes a quiet guest," Isabella smiled as she stared at the girls. "When you are finished, leave your plates here. I will clean up and store the rest of your buns and gelato for tomorrow. This afternoon, you may explore Taormina. I'm sure Marco can guide you around if you wish. The beach, if that interests you, is only a short distance down the hill. I need you back here by four o'clock to start dinner."

Marco turned towards the women, as Isabella excused herself.

"Would you like to join me in my shop? It is only a short distance from here. I can show you how to make glass just like my ancestors."

"I'd be interested." Olivia tried her best to sound unenthused, but genuinely cultural experiences had always excited her.

"I had actually planned on checking out one of the hotel spas. Do you have a recommendation?" Kate had looked forward to a spa day since she had stepped off the plane in Palermo. Pampering was exactly what she needed.

"I may stick around here actually, Isabella if

that's OK. I need to be near my phone in case my son calls. He needs my help with some school thing." Martha was a bit timid with her news, but she couldn't help but smile at the same time.

CHAPTER 13

A little later, Kate, Olivia, and Marco said their goodbyes to the others as they rushed out the door to begin their Taormina adventure.

Alone together, Isabella turned to her guest, "It's a rare treat for me to have a friend around for the day. Most students want to escape on their vacation, not stay here. Is it an emergency?"

Martha considered her words. *An emergency?* It wasn't something she needed to fly home over, but hearing Kurt yearn for his mother was so different and unique for her. The last time she could remember him needing her help was when he first started high school almost five years ago.

"No, not an emergency as such, but he needs my help. You know what it's like to be a mom. You're always on call!" Her chipper voice floated with her words.

"How old is your son?" Isabella asked as she and Martha began clearing the table of the remaining breakfast dishes.

"Kurt's nineteen. Just started college, but it sounds like he got in trouble with some of the rules, and needs my help getting out of a jam."

"I see." The older woman kept her head down, focusing on tidying up the table. "Before you go off to make your phone calls, would you like to help me set up some lunch?"

"I would love that." Martha lied. She wanted to be on the phone with the school as soon as possible. Preparing lunch when they'd just finished breakfast couldn't be farthest from her mind.

Isabella went to her fridge, taking out a platter of uncut meats.

"When my sons were younger, all they wanted was meat, meat, meat. Lamb, pig, cow, goat… whatever they could get their hands on.

I would say to them 'One day, you will need to make your own meat.' So I would have them go down to the butcher and watch him work. Now, my oldest owns a butcher shop in Agrigento where my youngest works. Best in the town!" She began slicing the meat into thin circles using a large silver carving knife.

"My second son, though, he never wanted to go. He'd stay at home or sneak away from his brothers. He would watch the others and think that he would always be provided for. When he left home to work at the docks, he would write to me about how horrible the food was. Complain, complain, complain. I blame myself for that." Her body shuddered for a second.

Martha looked at her curiously. "Why would you blame yourself?"

Isabella sighed as she finished up. "I always thought, maybe like a fool, that he could rely on his brothers or me if he needed to. But I'm getting older; there's no doubt about that! And his brothers are grown men with families of their own. They have their own children to teach their trade."

Martha watched as Isabella spread the slices

of meat she had cut onto a platter of thin brown crackers and golden-coloured cheeses.

But instead of a celebrated Italian chef, she watched another mother twenty or so years older than herself, suffer just as she did.

The woes of motherhood crossed every generation and every border.

For both Martha and Isabella, the thought of releasing a child not fully prepared for the realities of life was immeasurably frightening.

Martha thought back to the satisfaction she felt this morning hearing Kurt plead the words "mom" and "help" because he knew - he knew that she would jump to his side, hold his hand once again.

But, as Isabella said, maybe he would have to learn to make his own mistakes. He could not always rely on her to help him.

And likewise, she realised, chastened, she should not wish for her children to remain as they once were: needy and helpless.

With sadness in her eyes, but fire in her belly, Martha understood what she had to do.

"Isabella, I think I *am* going to go down to the beach today. Can you tell me how to get there?"

Isabella smiled as she offered to pack Martha a small lunch for her day in the sun.

CHAPTER 14

The light in Taormina was almost overwhelming.

Between the white and dusty browns of the stone walls and steps down to the gleaming blues of the ocean, the town itself had an opulent glow.

Olivia was almost too overwhelmed by the sheer beauty of it to care about the tourists and the hawking vendors that spread themselves throughout the streets. Normally, this wouldn't be her scene at all. But today, she was oblivious. Today, she was in love.

Marco had doted on her since leaving Kate at a nearby hotel spa. His tour of the city was fascinating as he pointed out the charming cathedrals and ancient ruins of the Greeks and Egyptians that remained behind.

Taking a detour, he insisted emphatically that the two make a stop at his favourite place in the city, the Giardini della Villa Comunale.

"What is that? More ruins?" she quizzed him.

"No, not at all. It's a park. The best park in the world."

"Why do you say that? How many parks have you been to that you can declare it as the best?" She smugly reminded him of her international knowledge.

"You know, you do not need to go everywhere to know that someplace is the best," Marco replied easily. "Sometimes, you just know, in your heart, that you do not need to search any further than what is right in front of you."

He stopped walking and turned towards her, offering his hand. It was such an unexpectedly gentlemanly gesture that Olivia was a bit taken aback. Almost without thinking, she gingerly placed her small white palm into his, allowing him to squeeze a bit.

The two walked the rest of the way in a

blissful silence, hand in hand, as they entered the park's grounds. Marco guided her expertly through the greenery, pointing out the remains of the old city zoo, and the base of the stone of Lazarus pagodas that jutted out almost as naturally as the trees and other flora.

"Can you see why I think that this is the best park?"

Olivia nodded eagerly as Marco spun her around towards the outside walls. She could instantly spot the reason as the trees disappeared and the Ionian Sea opened up before her.

The panoramic view allowed her to look down at the red and brown brick roofs of the buildings of Taormina with widened eyes and a fuller heart.

She had seen some resplendent views on her travels, but this was truly one of the most impressive ones. As she spun again, she spotted the tip of Mt. Etna peaking at her from a distance.

After a moment of taking in the salty sea air and listening to the breeze drift in the Italian pine trees, she turned back to her companion.

"While I see why you love this place, I have

to ask. Why would you not want to go out and see if this truly is the best park in the world? Are you not curious?"

"Of course I am!" He laughed without mocking. "But Taormina will always be home. It may not be Central Park or have the Eiffel Tower in the background, but it will have my heart, and I want to be where my heart is."

His words shot through her. Of course, she had many times heard the saying *Home is where the heart is*, but she had always put little faith in it. Her heart had always been wherever her suitcase was. Sure, it was a little battered and beaten from the road, but she had managed to keep it from heartbreak and sorrow. It was full of experiences, not love, and she was fine with that. Or at least, she hoped she was.

"What about you Olivia? Where is your heart? What place is your *villa comunale*?"

She sunk into deep thought as she retraced her travel memories, all of which were now a blur of deadlines and rewrites.

As a travel writer, her stories from the road were dissected and dismantled by people other than herself. Her photos and notes were just keepsakes until she had moved on. She had little time to actually take in a moment, let alone find the unique treasure of it. "I don't know if I've found it yet," she admitted. "Is that a bad?"

"You'll find it," Marco said, giving her a reassuring smile, "but in the meantime, you can borrow this park." His playful brown eyes softened as they caught hers. It wasn't pity that she saw inside of them though; it was a powerful warmth and fortitude she had not experienced before.

She longed to let go of his hand and place hers onto his chest, just to feel if his heart was beating like hers, fast and in a rhythm all new.

But she didn't dare do so. Instead, Olivia turned back to the sea, content with taking this moment in.

CHAPTER 15

"Y ou've reached Ed O'Toole. I am unable to answer my phone at the moment. Please leave me your name and phone number, and I will get back to you as soon as possible. Cheers."

Beep.

"Hello, love. It's noon here in Taormina, and I'm pretty sure you're in the thick of things at work. I am assuming that is why you are not answering. I just wanted to let you know that I am fine. Well, I'm better than fine. This place is amazing, and Chef Isabella is, well … amazing too. She left sunflowers for us all this morning. How lovely is that? Anyway, we have the afternoon off, so I am going to a spa at this place her grandson recommended. I hope you're not too jealous. It would, of course, be better if you were here with me, but I understand why you are not. At least, I think I understand. I'm not sure. I …I really want to talk to you and tell you more. Will you ring me when you get back from lunch or when you're not so busy? Okay. I think that's all. I love you."

Kate felt instant regret settle over her. She had promised herself that morning that she wasn't going to call Ed or even worry about why his phone seemed to just ring and ring whenever she tried to get through.

Yet, here she was leaving him a long and rambling message whereby she practically confessed her frustrations and need to see him.

The thought of the spa had never sounded more appealing to her than this moment. Marco had been able to convince the best spa in Taormina to take her for the day. Though the Hotel Lusso already looked packed with guests wrapped in white downy robes and slippers, the manager guided her to a private room where he handed her an English menu of their offerings.

She carefully selected the stone massage

with Sicilian oils, a dip in the salt water pools, a manicure, and a pedicure. Many of these treatments were things Kate had always wanted to try, but the high price of the fertility treatments had kept her from indulging at home. Even a trip to the beauty salon would have triggered instant guilt that she was spending too much on herself and not on the future of her family.

But as the manager came back with towels, robes, and slippers, the need for self-deprivation melted off as Kate stripped down her layers of clothing. She removed her wedding ring last, placing it carefully in the safe assigned to her along with her still silent mobile phone.

CHAPTER 16

The orange umbrella Martha rested under glided back and forth gently in the wind, and the pink concoction the bartender at the beach had made her, was just what she needed to cool her nerves. Stretching a seemingly endless distance, the pale sand and pebbles of Letojanni beach beckoned her and the hundreds of other sunbathers surrounding her, to give in to its charms.

She had never been one for the beach. When the children were young, she and William took regular family trips to the shore in the summer months. But as a mom, she considered those vacations more like business trips: there was always sunscreen to apply to someone's nose, and sandwiches to protect from sand and bugs. Her time to relax was more or less limited to the moments in which her husband would distract the children long enough for her to take a nap or read a chapter of a book.

But today, Martha was without worry or care. On the ride in on the beach bus, she had left a message for Kurt basically telling him that there was little she could do from Italy and that he would need to deal with it as a man.

She hated doing it, but she understood that she needed to let him stand on his own two feet. It wasn't as though freshman drinking exploits were anything new to a college principal - or indeed serious - and certainly nothing she needed to get involved with.

Anyway, a little scare like that would only stand her son in good stead for the remainder of his time in college.

So Martha decided, for the rest of this trip, a trip given to her as a means of escape from her children, she was off the grid.

And on her first day as a free woman for the first time in almost thirty years, she went to take a swim in the Ionian sea.

While all the other women her age sat dry and baking, she boldly removed her cover-up and marched herself into the sea.

The waves gathered and nipped gently at her legs, and the saltwater frothed and foamed around her body as she waded deeper in.

She dipped her head back, soaking her hair in the aquamarine sea, and eventually, she placed her whole body in, letting it rise to the surface to float lazily on her back.

As Martha stared up at the cloud-speckled sky, with a weight off her shoulders, suddenly the world seemed to open up to her like never before, and she imagined all of the other seas and oceans she could experience now.

She imagined herself trekking in Brazil, diving in Egypt, and snorkelling in Australia.

It was all so new and fresh.

A dream that was once her husband's, to travel and explore, had now taken over and become her own.

CHAPTER 17

*K*ate blew quickly on her nails, attempting to speed-dry them as she hurried up the stone steps back to Isabella's home. She was late—almost twenty minutes now—and hadn't had time to wait for the blue light machines to work their magic.

So instead, she ran, hoping to keep her freshly painted pink fingernails safe from harm.

She wasn't late on purpose. In fact, she had been watching the time meticulously, acutely aware of her obligation to be back at the villa for dinner preparations. But instead, it was the hotel manager that had kept her back. As she had requested the bill for her day at the spa, he had insisted that she had already paid.

"*Signor*," Kate explained, "there must be some mistake. I haven't paid for anything, and I am in a hurry. Can you just process a bill for me so I can pay and be on my way?" Her impatience was growing thin and the benefits of her relaxing day quickly wearing off.

The manager's thin moustache twitched as he looked her over.

"*Signorina* O'Toole," he explained, "I am telling you that your bill is already paid. You are free to go whenever you need."

"I don't understand," she countered impatiently, "How can that be possible? I haven't even given you my credit card!" She curtly handed him her Bank of Ireland debit card, insisting that he take it. The man's hands rose quickly as if to guard him from it, and she finally sighed and gave up, returning the card to her purse. "Fine. I will take my *free* day at the spa then..."

She waited for him to reply, but he instead walked from behind the long birchwood desk and graciously walked her to the door. "I hope you enjoyed your stay," he called, "Please do visit us again."

As she strolled along the cobblestone path outside the hotel, she found herself at a loss, wondering what to make of the situation.

Would another less charitable employee track her down later to try to get more money out of her than she owed?

Just in case, she sped up a bit, attempting to retrace her steps from earlier in the day when Marco had shown her the way to the hotel.

Rounding the corner, she spotted Martha, who brushed a patch of yellow sand from her skirt with a pink-tinged hand.

"Kate! Were you at this hotel?" the older woman gushed, running up to her. "Did you check out the beach at all? It was to die for."

"I thought you were staying back at the villa?" she replied distractedly. "Did you get everything sorted with your son?"

"No," Martha admitted, "but that's the thing, I figured that if I am on vacation, I should actually *be* on vacation. So, instead, I spent the entire day at the beach drinking these pink little cocktails and reading this brilliant book I picked up from the library back home. I totally lost track of time!"

"That sounds great," Kate smiled, pleased to see her looking so happy. "I spent my day at the spa here. For some reason, there was an issue with my bill, but I guess it worked itself out."

She didn't dare tell Martha that her opulent day of me-time was apparently on someone else's account.

The two women instead spent the rest of their quick walk back to Isabella's villa recounting their day, from the pedicurist who spoke nine languages to the bartender at the beach who purred at Martha while calling her "carina."

Olivia was already back at the villa.

Still glowing from her day in the sunlight, she moved around the kitchen effortlessly as she worked on her assigned recipe.

Marco walked her through a new, more efficient technique for chopping up tomatoes. Both stood arm and arm, sharing laughs and long glances.

Joining them at their workstations, Martha and Kate couldn't help but raise eyebrows at the pair of them, a budding couple if ever there was one, Kate thought.

As they made their sincerest apologies for being late, Isabella quickly handed them their handwritten recipe cards and dinner tasks of the evening.

Kate had the *secondo*, a swordfish chop, while Martha was assigned the *primo*, a most famous Sicilian recipe, the *pasta alla norma.*

Marco would make the dessert, a Sicilian version of cannoli.

Fluttering between stations, Isabella guided each woman with their dishes. She tasted everything, savouring even the simplest of spice combinations. When assisting Kate with chopping the swordfish into smaller pieces, she didn't flinch as she deftly added even more olive oil to the pot.

All the while as the dishes cooked, she hummed a sweet tune while pointing out opportunities for what she called "vista breaks" to take in the sight of the sun floating lower into the sea.

Occasionally, she stopped for lessons. For Martha, she applauded her instinct to double the garlic cloves to the pasta's already flavorful palate. Looking over Kate's seafood dish, she reminded the women that patience is a virtue. Cooking meat on low was sometimes the only way to get the best results.

And for Olivia, she reassured her that perfection wasn't necessary in a dish's appearance; and that sometimes, the look of a meal was deceptive with the worst tasting often being the most eye-catching.

As the group finished their final touches, Isabella gave her last lesson of the night on the virtue of wines.

None of the women admitted to being big fans or frequent drinkers, giving Isabella time to speak.

"Most of you probably only serve one wine per meal," she explained, "but in Sicily, we know that not every meal will have its perfect pair for each dish. Instead, we drink a glass with each course. For tonight, we have Olivia's *arancinette*. Deep-fried rice balls probably don't seem like any match for a wine, but every meal has its mate. The heaviness of it calls for something red, light, and full of flavour. Martha's pasta needs something to balance, rather than to detract, so a simple table red that is low on acidity is best. And finally, with Kate's sword-fish, we will drink a glass of Inzolia, a white grape wine."

"That's a ton of wine!" Kate exclaimed as she held her first glass high while Isabella poured a generous helping of the first red. "How does anyone stay sober in this country?"

"We drink slow and savour," Isabella smiled. "It would be a waste to drink too fast and spoil our food. With nowhere else to go and good company, who would want to spend their time too ill to take in the fun?

Marco gestured to the open doors leading out to the patio overlooking the seafront. The group followed, bringing their plates out to the main patio for an *al fresco* experience. Isabella too had brought out a handful of small table candlesticks to illuminate the white linen tablecloth and the shimmering blue ceramic dinnerware.

CHAPTER 18

The evening air was light and fragrant.

While the lights of Taormina glittered, and the sounds of people on the street filled the night, the tranquillity of it all gave the scene an almost out-of-body atmosphere.

In her mind, Olivia recognized it as one of the most authentic travel moments she had experienced in years. It was free from obligation and pretence and as natural as sitting with her own family.

Her heart ached as she remembered that there would only be one more dinner like this.

With her wine glass raised, she instinctively stood, turning towards the front of the table where Marco and Isabella sat, "To our host. To this beautiful, mythical town. To new friends. To new hopes and dreams. To life and food."

"*Cent'ann!*" Marco chimed in, tapping her glass with his. "100 hundreds of life and love!"

"*Cin Cin!*" followed Isabella joyfully as she looked over her table. The group dived into their meal ravenously; the mixture of the swordfish, pasta, and rice warming over their senses and awakening their tired minds.

Isabella talked endlessly about the tucked-away Taormina vineyards she travelled to for their drinks and her favourite vendor at the docks who always gave her the best deal on her seafood when the market was low.

"Isabella, what do you do when you are not hosting your cookery course? Do you spend the time alone in this big home?" Martha asked with genuine curiosity.

"Oh no! I go out on friends' boats. I travel to see friends. I tend to my garden. And some-times, I have my sons or grandsons take me dancing."

"Dancing?" Kate's eyes lit up. Before she married Ed, she had loved to go to local night-clubs and discos.

"Of course! There are several dance halls here. And sometimes, I'll even go to the modern clubs along the beach for young people. But that is when I am feeling my bravest."

Marco laughed, "You should see her! I've taken her to several beach bars and she will ask anyone to dance. She especially likes the men with longer hair... right, Grandma?"

Isabella gently brushed him off with a wave of her hands as she stood to go retrieve the desserts from the fridge.

Kate continued, "I would love to go dancing tonight if we could. Where would you recommend, Marco?"

"I would say Passaggi. It's a good mix of not too young, and not too old. And it's very romantic being out on the main square. Plus, the drinks are always strong. I could take you if you would like."

"Seriously, would you? That would make my night!" Kate clapped her hands excitedly and bounced like a child in her chair. "How about you, Olivia and Martha? Will ye come?"

Martha readily answered yes, excited to

continue on her adventure from earlier in the day.

Olivia, on the other hand, was reticent. She had spent all day with Marco, and she found him becoming less of a character for her travel article and more of a fixture in her own mind. Venturing out with him in such a charged environment might well push her in a way she wasn't exactly ready for.

However, she also knew that seeing some of Taormina's nightlife was almost essential to getting the city's entire profile. She had learned early on in her days on the road that what a town may appear to be in the day could change in an instant when the sun went down.

This was her shot to capture the entire experience.

CHAPTER 19

The four quickly demolished their cannoli along with the final wine of the night, a syrupy sweet *passitos.* The women then went back into their rooms, changing into more formal attire.

Kate chose a black halter dress with a plunging neckline. Martha stuck with her long, golden maxi dress and a black sweater over her shoulders.

Olivia spent the most time preparing, as she rummaged through her backpack for the pearly white shift dress she had picked up in Barcelona several years back.

She paired the look with the teardrop

earrings a friend from Tokyo had gifted her, and a quick dab of ruby red lipstick - a rare luxury she typically didn't indulge in while on the road.

Marco and the others waited for her down the terrace stairs near the front entrance.

His eyes lit up at the sight of her descending the steps. She had swept up her blonde hair in a slightly messy ballerina bun atop her head, revealing her dainty neck and the slight curve of her bare, lean back.

The light from the villa bounced off her white dress, almost giving her a halo as she glided down to meet Marco's outstretched arm.

As the group approached the town, the sounds of music, laughter, and shouting grew closer. Taking a prominent place right in the centre of Taormina, right then it looked oddly part of the scenery, with its open-air tables, and white and tan linen awnings.

Locals and tourists mingled, chatting amongst each other on the tan sofas and huddled in secluded, corner tables.

The music was a mixture of standard club songs with thumping bass and vibrating lyrics to softer, more traditional Italian standards sung by crooners with booming voices.

Young couples danced dangerously close, locking their bodies to one another as they swayed with the beat. Older men and women sat circled the dance floor, watching and pointing at the movements. When the music would suddenly, almost disjointedly, switch to a familiar tune, they would jump up effortlessly, weaving through the younger dancers to find their place in the centre with their partners.

Kate watched one older couple contentedly.

The man, hunched over from age, removed his grey cap to reveal a wisp of waspy, thinning hair. He reached for his partner, a woman of equal age and stature, and guided her slowly out to the floor where they danced as they must have twenty, thirty, maybe even forty years before. Cheek to cheek, they swayed, not even whispering a word - both sets of eyes closed firmly as if they were picturing another scene from when they danced years before.

A twinge of guilt overcame her as she remembered her first dance with Ed at their wedding. She could almost feel him cupping her back with his large hand, guiding her to the centre of the empty floor. When their song ended, he dipped her dramatically back with such ease and poise.

And at this moment, now at the Taormina club, she couldn't help but wish he was there with her, dancing like this couple, too full of memories and moments to care about the present.

Martha noticed the pained look on her dewy face. As Olivia and Marco slipped off to the bar to gather the drink orders, she asked her new friend, "Are you all right?"

"Just thinking about my husband. I haven't heard from him since yesterday when he was too busy to talk. He never called me back, and he hasn't answered the phone yet." She felt a bit foolish to be talking about her marriage problems.

Martha placed her hands tenderly on Kate's.

"That's too bad. He's the one missing out though, not you. There were so many things my husband missed out on when he became too wrapped up in life—first moments with the kids, day trips to visit our friends, opportunities like this… But, in the end, I guess it's the quality of time spent, not quantity. While it is amazing to have a partner to share things with, sometimes, it's best to be our own companion."

Kate nodded, understanding her words. She was her own companion here in Sicily, and it was time to start enjoying and loving herself.

Suddenly, the music switched over as an oldie, a popular American dance song came on.

She grinned as she tugged on Martha's hand.

"Well, since you and me are own companions tonight, we might as well partner up on the dance floor."

"$\mathcal{M}$arco, look." Olivia tapped on her companion's shoulders attempting to gain his attention. She pointed at Kate and Martha as they jumped and spun around on the dance floor. Their careless, uninhibited dance moves had gained attention as both young and old infectiously joined in around them.

Olivia laughed as an older man dressed completely in white reached for Martha's raised hand and spun her body into his. Martha dipped her head back and laughed as she greeted her new partner fearlessly.

Kate had also gained the attention of several young Italian men, but she continued to dance by herself, her black dress blowing in the breeze as she twirled and dipped to the rhythm of the music.

"They look happy," Marco shouted over the music, handing Olivia the drinks. He led her back to their table near the exit. Compared to the stuffy interior and the shuffle of sweaty, youthful bodies, the terrace's nearly empty chairs and tables were a relief.

"So, what did you order me?" She stared at her orange-ish red drink with orange rinds floating near the top.

"Negroni. It's like a burnt orange gin martini with a twist. It's my favourite."

"If this is your favourite, then what are you drinking?" She glanced at his pale pink drink.

"Bellini, of course. But actually, I thought if you did not like yours, we could always trade. The bellini is a little more gentle." He eyed her laughingly.

"Gentle?" She pretended to be taken aback, "I've had saki with samurais and whiskey with the Irish. I can certainly handle this." With that, she lifted her glass to her mouth and carelessly sucked back the liquor. The gin was sour and almost tart and her face puckered in reaction and she coughed a bit into her hand.

Marco laughed at her as he spun his glass in his hand.

The music slowed to a melodic waltz.

Martha and Kate bounded from the crowd, shaking with laughter and excitement. They found their chairs next to Olivia and Marco as they continued their conversation. "—he didn't speak a word of English, but I'm pretty sure whatever he was saying to me wasn't exactly romantic!" Martha's face was a bright pink as she raised her champagne to the sky "To Taormina men!"

"I will certainly toast to that," chimed in Marco meeting her glass with his own.

"Olivia, are you going to dance? I'll join you once I catch my breath if you like?" Kate panted a bit, not even turning to face her. She was focused on getting back onto the dance floor.

"I'm not that much of a dancer actually. I once broke my foot in a disco in Thailand. I prefer to sit back and watch."

"Well, that's unacceptable," Marco insisted,

"you have to dance." He gently yanked at her arm till she could no longer protest.

She glanced back at the others, unsure of what to do; Martha shooed her away and Kate just smiled, knowingly.

Olivia turned her gaze up to Marco. "I'm not much of a slow dancer either," she said, feeling like she was repeating herself. "I'm not even sure how to do this."

Marco stood arms-length from her, towering over her petite frame.

"Just take my hand," he said. She tentatively offered hers, and he lifted it shoulder level, pulling her slightly towards his deceptively muscular frame as they headed back out to the dance area.

SWAYING TOGETHER TO THE MUSIC, his hand went around the crook of Olivia's back, and she could feel his body moving tenderly and slowly. Her right hand found its way to his chest, and she mindlessly toyed with the black buttons on his shirt.

His head arched down to lean on the side of hers. She took in his scent, warm and sweet, almost like a mixture of ginger and exotic fruit. His hand felt rough from years working in his trade, yet it wasn't any less soothing as they fell into a trance.

"I was thinking about our conversation earlier at the park," he said softly into her ear.

"Mhmm" she whispered, not fully paying attention to his words.

"I've decided that it isn't my favourite place anymore." Olivia glanced up at him, unsure of why he was suddenly bringing this up. "You are. I mean, I want you to be. I want you to be my place."

The two came to a stop, now standing at the far corner of the stone-tiled floor. She looked back at him, releasing her hand from his chest. "I don't understand."

"Can you stop looking, stop searching for your perfect place?" He lifted her chin to meet his eyes as he bent down a little to be face-to-face with her. "Olivia..." Marco's mouth met hers, gentle and firm. He grasped both arms around her waist making for an impossible escape, yet she didn't struggle. Her arms twisted around his neck and into the soft brown threads of his hair.

After a long few seconds, the lights and the sounds of the thundering feet on the tile knocked her back into reality.

Marco instantly sensed the change as well, as she moved away from him, taking two steps backwards.

"I know that it is very soon. I know that you have a life, a job on the other side of the world, but I cannot let you leave tonight without asking you to think about it. Please?"

"I ... uh, I have to go. Tell the others I'm feeling ill, okay?"

She spun around on her heel, leaving Marco standing alone on the packed dance floor. The crowd formed around him, sucking him into the scene of Taormina as Olivia made her escape out of the club and back onto the stone steps leading to the villa.

The starry evening and the lanterns from the streets, broke through her whirling thoughts and confusion, guiding her home.

CHAPTER 21

The following morning, Kate once again woke to the sound of silence.

No phone calls, no email pings, nothing. But for whatever reason, she wasn't perplexed or upset over it.

Instead, she took it as a sign that life was as it should be. Plus, after a night like hers, she was grateful to be without interruption to process the raging headache and dizzy spells that overwhelmed her.

Moving a bit slower than usual, she went about her morning routine and joined the rest of the class downstairs.

Martha was assisting Isabella with the pastry recipe they had made the day before, while Olivia was wrapped up on the couch, typing away furiously on her laptop. She briefly registered Kate's presence and went back to her determined work.

"*Buongiorno!*" Isabella greeted Kate excitedly at the entrance to the kitchen. "It's certainly good to see you out and about. Martha has told me all about your night on the town."

Kate looked down and laughed lightly at the flour-caked handprint Isabella had left on her shirt. "Can I help with breakfast?" she asked.

"Of course! Olivia learned how to make the Sicilian version of Bloody Marys, and Martha is making the briosce. You can make the eggs in a tomato sauce. Simple recipe, but it's tricky."

She went to the bowl in the corner of the room where a stack of brown eggs sat. She then had Kate follow her into the pantry where she stored all of her homemade tomato sauces and pastes.

"How do you know which one is which?" Kate asked. "They all look the same to me." There had to be over a hundred clear jars full of red, chunky sauces lining the walls of her back room.

"Easy. I try them." Isabella pulled out a spoon from her apron and slowly began tasting each sauce, one by one. "I make these in the winter with my grandchildren. They each make two or three of their favourite recipes. Sometimes I write their name on the lid, but it wears off and I have trouble remembering who made what." About a quarter of the way through, she stopped, grabbing the one she had last tasted.

They returned to the kitchen where Martha had just placed her pastries in the oven. Both women gathered round as Isabella showed them the proper way to crack an egg, and the right temperature to cook sunny-side up. Once the shape of the egg started to take form and the white was showing, Isabella gently added spoonfuls of blood-red sauce. Adding diced peppers, onions, and a bit of feta cheese, she expertly flipped the egg over with such ease the others let out a small gasp.

Kate took over the next one. Following each of the steps, she mimicked Isabella's movements and instructions precisely. But when it came time to flip, she hesitated nervously and the egg slipped off of her spatula and back onto the pain making a chaotic mess of vegetables, yolk, and sauce.

Defeated, she turned towards the chef unsure of how to proceed.

"No problem. We'll scramble this one." Isabella walked her through the steps to puree the egg mixture without burning.

"Even in our messiest mistakes, we can find beauty." The chef handed Kate a fork and encouraged her to try a taste of the scrambled egg. The sensation of the runny egg was marvellous as it mixed with the spicy, peppery flavour of the sauce. All Kate could do was give her food a giant thumbs up and she attempted to swallow.

The rest of the women joined in around Kate's station, not bothering to sit at the communal table. The briosce finished soon after and Isabella retrieved the remained of yesterday's gelato. Olivia's Sicilian Bloody Mary was the perfect follow-up. For Kate, breakfast was enough to wake her from her stupor and put her back in the real world.

Olivia however, was in her own little world, oblivious to all that was around her.

The night's romantic twist with Marco had

her reeling. Sure, she'd had flirtations and even boyfriends while travelling. But none had been serious. No one had certainly ever asked her to stay or to even consider it. There would be promises to write, some video chats, and even gift exchanges, but eventually, the long distance relationships would unravel, leaving her in a mess of emotions.

But what Marco had said last night was completely different. He wasn't asking her to travel with him in mind. He wasn't asking for a long-distance relationship, a couple of phone calls here and there. He was asking her to stay here in Taormina. It was a proposition that terrified and, suspiciously, excited her. Especially as he had been so forthright and so honest, given what little time they'd spent together. *I want you to be my place.*

She had spent all night going over his words, and most of the morning going through her work, analyzing her last steps as she travelled.

She made a pros and cons list and wrote late-night emails to a couple of trusted friends. She even opened up her secret travel journal, a notebook in which she kept all of her true feelings regarding her life on the road.

Instead of glossing over the bad or making it more editorial or readable, she put it out on the line. And the words seemed to be saying that while life on the road was a joy, there was obviously something missing.

Maybe that piece of the puzzle was someone special, someone with whom to share that joy?

CHAPTER 22

*A*s the breakfast lesson finished up, and Isabella gave the women instructions to be back by 3 pm for dinner, the women dispersed to their afternoon activities.

Kate and Martha planned on shopping at some of the boutiques in the town. But for Olivia, hunting for new dresses or a pair of shoes was nowhere near what she had planned on doing.

She instead rushed out of the villa and towards Taormina in search of Marco's glass shop. She had found the address online, but navigating the streets was much more difficult than she had considered. She jogged past the medieval fortresses and cathedrals full of picture takers and tour guides and the children playing football in the narrow, shadowed alleyways.

Eventually, she found her street and instinctively took a left. She sped up as she spotted the sign for Marco's glassware shop, almost running to the entrance.

But the doorway of the red and white store was locked.

Olivia knocked loudly, hoping that someone would hear her.

Her heart deflated with each unanswered knock. "Marco?" she called out, frantically looking into the shop. "Marco," she called out again. Still no reply. A crowd of nosy Italian men and women gathered around her, all curious as to the strange tourist shouting at the empty shop.

And then, she heard the door heave and the chains unlock. A tired, haggard-looking Marco answered. She ducked under his arm and inside.

"What's wrong? What is it?" He guided Olivia to a row of red chairs in the corner of the gallery. She hadn't even taken a second to look at the beautiful glass wares and sparkling vases. She was instead fixed on Marco. He was wearing a dusty rubber apron and gloves. His work pants were frayed at the bottom and his grey shirt was tattered and full of paint and acid marks.

"You were working—" she said, while catching her breath, "I shouldn't have—" Olivia shook her head in irritation with herself, feeling silly and childish. What on earth had possessed her?

"It's nothing," he insisted. "But what is wrong? Why are you here? I thought that after last night, you would—" Marco couldn't finish his words. Instead, he took to his knees in front of her. He removed his gloves and placed them next to her. His hands cupped Olivia's as she fidgeted with her thumbs.

"I didn't run from you because of what you did or said. I ran from you because ... I was afraid. I ran from you because when you kissed me, I felt something I had never felt before. It's the reason why I never want to run again. I don't want to run from you, Marco. I want to stay here and give this a shot."

He stared at her, stunned and apprehensive.

He looked about the room, unsure if she was a figment of his imagination.

But Olivia couldn't wait any longer.

She took his scruffy face into her own small hands, cupping his jaw and cheekbones. His hair ruffled in her fingertips. Bending forward, she kissed him with such urgency she could feel her heartbeat rush to her head. Not letting go of their embrace, Marco scooped her up by the waist and picked her small frame off the chairs and into his arms. Her feet could only float above the tiled floor.

There they remained the rest of the morning, tightly coiled, neither daring to move.

CHAPTER 23

The outside world wasn't oblivious to the new couple.

Kate and Martha, amidst their shopping trip, had stumbled upon the quaint shop.

Recognizing the name above the door and recalling what Marco had said before about his line of business, they quickly deduced who the owner was. And by the looks of what was going on inside, he didn't look too prepared to open shop today.

"Oh to be young and in love again," Martha sighed as she and Kate moved onwards.

"It certainly reminds me of Ed and I when we were that young and naive." A tinge of sadness spiked Kate's words. "But I guess it all wears off eventually."

Martha stopped and faced her. "No, honey, it doesn't. The feeling may change, and yes, it may diminish. But that essential feeling, that feeling of tenderness and wanting doesn't just disappear overnight. To break down true love... well, that would take much more than a couple of fights."

"Did you and your husband have disagreements though? Did you ever feel him slipping away from you?"

"Of course, every married couple does. I felt like our relationship was slipping away many times, especially when money was tight or our children took too much of our time and energy. But we would always find one another in the storm, eventually. Even if it took months, sometimes years. The other one would be there—the answer to all the questions."

"Did I tell you why I am here - in Sicily?" Martha shook her head as Kate continued. "We can't conceive. We can't have a baby and it is my fault. My body doesn't want me to have a child, and Ed, well, he can't handle that. We've been trying everything, treatments, even considering surgery, and nothing. Now all he wants to do is break away from me, and all I want to do is run to him."

"Oh Kate, honey…" Martha's voice softened as large welts of tears trickled down Kate's face. She slumped onto the hot paved pathway against a smooth, yellow-painted building.

She sniffed as she continued. "My doctor told us to take a holiday to get away from it all. So I picked this place. Ed always wanted to see Italy. I thought he would jump on it. I had hoped we could reconnect. Now I can't even get him to answer my phone calls or texts. I'm not even sure what I am going home to after this. I'm so afraid that he won't be there." Her hands hid her eyes as her body shook, her confession pouring out of her.

"We have to have faith in the ones that we love," Martha reassured her. "We have to believe that they will do the right thing. We can't try to keep them or shelter them. Eventually, we need to set them free if that's what's necessary. And if Ed isn't there, if he's stupid enough to leave someone so amazing as you, then you're strong enough to see this through alone."

She encircled her arms around Kate's slim, pale shoulders, brushing the strands of flaxen hair from her hands and face. "Now honey, dry those tears and let's go and find some lunch. I'm sure Isabella would say that a good meal works wonders."

CHAPTER 24

"*I*sabella ...how do you pronounce this?" Martha studied her recipe card.

"Timballo Polizzano" Isabella enunciated the words slowly, accenting the hard "p."

It was later that evening, and all three students had returned to Isabella's villa in time for the dinner preparations. As always her recipe cards waited for them at their station.

But their ingredients were nowhere to be found.

"When do we begin making dinner?" Olivia's card displayed a recipe for a complex and intimidating prawn salad.

"Well, that's the surprise!" Isabella threw up

her hands as if she had practised this moment countless times before. "On my last dinner, I try to treat my new chefs to the most authentic Sicilian dinner I can think of. And that is why, instead of what is on those cards, we are spending the rest of the evening making …. pizza!" She beamed at them, her toothy, gapped smile widening as she awaited their reactions.

"Pizza? You're going to teach us how to make Italian pizza?" Kate, now feeling much better after confiding in Martha earlier, was thrilled. She had always wanted to learn how to toss and spin dough like pizza chefs in the movies.

"But, wait, why the recipe cards then?" Olivia was dubious, waiting for the other shoe to drop. She was extremely relieved to hear that they were making pizza though. Cooking fresh prawns had seemed way too much even for her.

Especially with the crazy mess her mind was in.

"They go in your books," said Isabella. "Check in the top shelf of your station. You'll find one for each of you."

Martha pulled hers out first. It was a tan

leather-bound photo album. In each of almost all the one hundred slots were recipes that Isabella had written out by hand. They were sorted and arranged by meal.

"Oh, this is beautiful." Kate carefully felt her own book, covered in blue vinyl with golden sunflowers blooming from the edges.

Olivia's was a fire engine red hardcover with a large strap to keep the pages intact.

Each woman placed their final recipe card in their new cookbook and shut the pages.

Returning their attention back to Isabella, she spoke again, "In Italy, we believe that the real pizza, the original pizza is from Naples. But because I do not have the proper oven, we will go into the town and learn from the experts."

THE OTHERS FOLLOWED her back into old Taormina where they stopped at a hidden corner *panifico.*

An older gentleman about Isabella's age slowly moved from around the corner and greeted her festively. He spoke Italian as Isabella translated, "This is Tomas. He is the owner of the bakery, and he welcomes you here today. He wants to let you know that he has been friends with my husband and me since pizza was first invented."

The women chuckled at the joke, as the two chefs stood arm in arm together. "He is going to walk you through making the dough for the Neapolitan, and then how to add the sauce and toppings."

The petite man silently led Kate, Olivia and Martha to the back of the tiny bakery, where mixing bowls and ingredients were already waiting. Pointing out each item, he walked the students through each step as Isabella translated tips and tricks he would occasionally shout out.

When it was time to spin the dough, the women watched in awe as he transformed a large ball of dough into a spinning, hypnotic wheel.

Olivia attempted to throw hers first, but it landed with a thud on the wooden table. Martha followed, and while she could catch it, the actual spinning alluded her. The only one that seemed to possess the ability to throw, spin, and mould the dough was Kate.

And even she was shocked at what came naturally.

The lesson was then followed by a taste test of various white and red sauces. Some chunky, others runny. Finally, Isabella talked to them about cheeses and why goat's cheese in Sicily was so important, pointing out that the region's cows were in short supply, and that in the summer, transporting non-hard cheeses like mozzarella was almost impossible for small vendors like Tomas. Instead, he improvised with goat's and harder cheeses.

As the three waited for the oven to finish warming their pizza, Marco slipped in the back entrance, greeting his grandmother first by handing her a small, note written on one of her recipe cards.

Isabella read it and then glanced back at her students who were chatting merrily over some red wine.

"Kate," Isabella called out and the Irish-woman duly joined the two in the corner of the store. "It seems like there is a change of plan for you this evening. Marco is going to take you to the docks. You have somewhere to be."

"What? What do you mean? I don't leave until tomorrow night."

"No, no, nothing like that. You're going on a boat trip around the bay. It departs in one hour, which gives you enough time to grab a change of clothing. Marco will see to it that you get to where you need to go."

"I don't understand..." Marco offered Kate his arm and escorted the dazed woman out of the bakery, as Isabella returned to the rest of the lesson.

CHAPTER 25

Without any more details other than that she needed to be on the docks by 8 pm, Marco was of no help to Kate.

He showed her back into Isabella's villa so that she could change into warmer clothing, and grab a sweater from her backpack, and then he rode with her in a taxi to the nearby town of Messina, where the main docks were.

He pointed out a large white yacht with the name *Mariano* painted in golden letters on its side. The captain, dressed in traditional sailor white and black chatted with Marco as he confirmed the details with him.

"Kate, this is Captain Alfonzo. He says your

companion is waiting and you will take off as soon as you are ready."

"I'm sorry, but I do not know what is going on. I don't have a com—" Her words cut off as she saw a figure ascend the stairs up from the yacht's cabin. "Ed!" Without thinking, she jumped down into the boat and ran towards her husband, catching him in a hug.

As she finally let go, he tentatively cried, "Surprise!"

"Surprise? I don't understand. How are you here? *Why* are you here?" The sight of her husband in Taormina was too overwhelming.

"I arrived on the flight after yours, and I've been here ever since. Didn't you get my flowers or wonder who paid for your insanely expensive spa day?"

Her mind whirling, Kate laughed as she put the pieces together.

"I wanted you to have the time of your life away from me and the pressure to conceive," Ed told her gently. "I had hoped this little break would be a way to bring you, the *real* you, back to me. But when I saw you crying on the path in town this afternoon, I knew it was time to let you in on the surprise." He stretched his arms out wide as if revealing his big moment.

"I never wanted to hurt you, love. I am so sorry for how I have acted and how I have pulled away from you. It was never my intention. Our adventure has just begun, whether we have kids or not. And this trip, watching you from a distance, I don't want to miss a moment of this journey with you ever again. Please forgive me."

"Ed—" the words caught in Kate's throat as she struggled to see him past the tears in her eyes. "I, I …" She struggled to find a response to his eloquent words. Instead, she chose to shout out, "I love you!"

He moved towards her, unable to contain his emotions anymore. As he kissed her, Kate could feel the passion and the romance that was once lost rekindle slowly like a new fire. It burned brighter this time and lasted far longer. Whatever had divided them had now brought them here, in Taormina, on the Ionian Sea together at last.

She knew that no matter the obstacles they faced, however long life had to give, she and Ed would never again be parted.

Behind the married couple, the yacht had left its place on the dock as the choppy green seas parted swiftly for its travels.

It floated quickly on, past the Sicilian island and its beautiful, glimmering bays. Ahead of them was only the sea with its endless possibilities, but neither was scared.

Instead, the two relaxed as their vessel chased the setting sun, putting all of their troubles behind them.

CHAPTER 26

SIX WEEKS LATER

*T*he red envelope addressed to her caught Isabella's eye.

It had been weeks since she'd received a personal letter, and intriguingly, this one was from an address in her town.

She quickly tore into it. But instead of finding a letter, she found a clipping from a glossy magazine.

It read:

A Taste of Sicily

By Olivia Bennett, Chief Travel Correspondent

When you have travelled for as long as I have and collected as many stories as postcards, cities and places - even those straight from legends and lore - pass as a blur.

And while the life of a perpetual nomad may seem appealing, it certainly has its downsides.

As a travel writer, for the most part, I have little say on where I go or what I will be doing. When Erica, our fearless editor assigned me a story set in Taormina, Sicily, I was hesitant. Sure, I've been to Italy before. I have seen the ancient Roman ruins and tasted authentic pizza. But unlike so many others, for me, that country has never felt much more than bricks and history, with great fashion thrown in as a bonus.

And for that reason, I begged not to write this article.

But now, here I am, in Taormina. Over three days in the spring, I stayed at a villa overlooking the Ionian Sea and the awe-inspiring beauty that is the central hub of Southern Sicily, Mount Etna.

(A friend once told me that Etna, a once powerful volcano, held all of the Italian native's infamous tempers...).

I came here to learn how to cook under the

guidance of Chef Isabella and to investigate why her skills and hospitality have gained almost a cult following amongst tourists and foodies.

I did learn how to cook, as well as shop for fresh produce, enjoy gelato for breakfast, and fearlessly chop swordfish. But more importantly, I walked away with more than just a cookbook full of handwritten recipes and friendships to last a lifetime.

I walked away with love.

That's right; fearless wanderer Olivia Bennett has developed not only a taste of - and for - Sicily, found love and settled down.

Taormina, the picturesque historical town located in eastern Sicily, has claimed me.

I should have realised it the moment I got off the bus from Palermo. The clear blue skies, the air that smelled like tomatoes and kumquat...this place was magical. Its residents with their wide grins, effervescent attitudes, and open hearts its magicians.

With each morsel of briosce and pasta from Isabella's Kitchen, I was becoming more and more Sicilian. And I was welcoming the change even as I pretended to resist it.

Then, one afternoon, a handsome Italian

called Marco took me on a tour of the city. We stopped at the public gardens and took in a panoramic view of the area. My companion had not travelled as much as I and had rarely been outside of his home country. Yet, he told me that he did not need to go anywhere to know that this park, the very one we stood in, was the best in the world all because it was home.

It was a corny sentiment I thought, one reserved for movies and cheap romances. But on another night, I found myself dancing cheek to cheek with the same man and wondering, "When have I ever felt so at home? Where have I ever felt so whole?" And suddenly, I knew that this man was right.

So many of us travel because we long to find better, more exciting places. And if you do it enough, you may just find it. I have.

Taormina is it, at least for me.

For some, it may indeed just be another tourist trap in the middle of the ocean, but you do not need to travel the world to know when your world is perfect as is. You do not need to perfect perfection (a lesson I learned very quickly from Chef Isabella).

That is why I have requested to stay here, in Sicily, for the time being at least.

I am giving my newfound home and love a chance. We will find our new chapter, our new dish, and our new park together. And I suspect will not need to go much further than Isabella's Villa to find them.

I hope you will continue to follow my journey as I, and my new fiance Marco, travel through Italy and the rest of the Mediterranean together.

Until my next correspondence, I wish you all happy travels.

Isabella placed the article down on her wooden table and took a deep breath. The kind words from her soon-to-be granddaughter-in-law had touched her more than she had anticipated.

To know that she had helped and inspired someone so deeply, had made the labours of her life worth it, in many ways.

But for now, she couldn't dwell on her part in the fate of Olivia—or of Kate, who had too recently written about a baby on the way.

Or even that of Martha who had taken it

upon herself to go on a year-long cruise around the world - alone.

Instead, Isabella had only enough time to focus on writing out tonight's recipe cards.

In a few hours, this large wooden table would again be surrounded by new visitors, eager to take advantage of her culinary knowledge and soak up her wisdom.

And perhaps inadvertently find what they were looking for right in her Taormina kitchen.

Escape to Italy Series

Escape to the Islands Series

AVAILABLE NOW

AVAILABLE NOW

145

Printed in Great Britain
by Amazon